T0243619

SURVIVE and KEEP SURVIVING

Mel Mallory

An imprint of Enslow Publishing

WEST 44 BOOKS™

**Please visit our website, www.west44books.com.
For a free color catalog of all our high-quality books,
call toll free 1-800-398-2504.**

Cataloging-in-Publication Data

Names: Mallory, Mel.
Title: Survive and keep surviving / Mel Mallory.
Description: New York : West 44, 2022. | Series: West 44 YA verse
Identifiers: ISBN 9781978595927 (pbk.) | ISBN 9781978595910
(library bound) | ISBN 9781978595934 (ebook)
Subjects: LCSH: Children's poetry, American. | Children's poetry,
English. | English poetry.
Classification: LCC PS586.3 M355 2022 | DDC 811'.60809282--dc23

First Edition

Published in 2022 by
Enslow Publishing LLC
29 East 21st Street
New York, NY 10011

Editor: Caitie McAneney
Designer: Katelyn E. Reynolds

Photo Credits: Cvr (watercolor background) Oksana
Telesheva/Shutterstock.com; cvr, p. 1 (hand drawn font)
Azuzl/Shutterstock.com.

Printed in the United States of America

CPSIA compliance information: Batch #CW22W44: For further information contact
Enslow Publishing LLC, New York, New York at 1-800-398-2504.

for the survivors who have shown me softness

DAMAGE

Years ago, my paranoia
and delusions grew

like an invasive plant
in my mom's garden,

with vines that trailed
throughout our house

and coursed through
the entire town.

WEEDS

Psychosis wrecked
everything in its path,
and now all I can do
is weed the garden.

Apologize, smile, and
keep my head down.

But what happens
if the roots of the plant
are still buried?

What does *recovery* mean
if the plant
grows back?

PSYCHO

It's the end of seventh period.
I'm still thinking about
what Kendall Wilson said.

At lunch, I slipped
and spilled French fries
on her jacket. Ketchup
sprayed everywhere.

I'm so sorry, I mumbled
and looked away.
It was an accident.

She smiled. But I could
tell she was mad.

*Just don't go all
psycho on me,* she said.

AFTER SCHOOL

I drive to Dr. Lewis's office
seven miles away,
between a nail salon and café.

I can smell traces of
burnt coffee and rubbing alcohol
from inside his waiting room.

The receptionist greets me.
Good afternoon, Mara.

I don't even have to sign in.
She knows me. I'm a regular.

PSYCHOSIS 101: LESSON ONE

In this very office,
I learned all about
psychosis.

psy · cho · sis
noun

Dictionary
definition:

A mental condition
that causes you
to lose touch
with reality.

You might hear,
see, or believe things
that others don't.

Many people
fully recover.

But other times,
symptoms lie low,
ready to
attack again.

DR. LEWIS'S OFFICE

His smooth white walls
are covered in posters.

Men climbing mountains and
ballerinas pointing their toes.

Each poster comes with
its own cheesy quote.

Believe in yourself!
Never give up!

> I'd rather be surrounded
> by blank walls.

> No mountain men.
> No ballerinas.

REPLAY

I tell Dr. Lewis
what Kendall said.
He raises his eyebrows
and leans forward.
Rests his bearded chin
on one hand.
He asks if she's my friend.
I shake my head.

*So why does it matter
what she thinks?*
I stare at his blue button-down shirt.
He never wears a coat or tie.
(My dad once said
he dresses unprofessionally,
as if it matters.)

I shrug, but
Kendall's words still
replay in my head.

Like a bad commercial
on a steady loop.
I wonder if she
thinks I'm crazy,
like everyone else did
back in ninth grade,
when they whispered,
She's psychotic!

HOME

Dad watches TV from the couch.

Mom scrubs dishes
in the kitchen sink.
She looks up as I
close the front door
and kick off my shoes.

Her short hair
sticks up in the back.
Her lips look chapped,
like she's been
biting them.

How was school?

Fine.

And Dr. Lewis?

Good.

We both don't know
what else to say.

I disappear upstairs
to avoid another
staring competition.

MODEL HOMES

When I was a kid,
Mom would
take me to work
where she decorated
model homes.

She said there was
a science behind
angling the furniture.
Draping the curtains.

Making each room
feel like part of
the perfect home.

RULES

Mom wants our house
to look just as good as the
rooms she decorates for work.

Our house rules:

If you use the kitchen,
you must wash the dishes
right away.

If you pick a book off
the shelf, you must put it
back in the right order.

If you drop a hand towel
on the floor, you must
replace it with a fresh one.

Everything must appear
like no one actually
lives here.

ORDER

Last month,
Mom put plastic wrap
over the couches so they
wouldn't get scratched.

Dad couldn't help
but roll his eyes.

*You're out of
your mind, Julie.
It's just a sofa.*

But Mom doesn't care
if he complains.
As long as he doesn't put
his feet on the table.

BEDROOM

I prefer to be in
my bedroom,
away from
my mom's rules,
my dad's irritation.

In my room,
the walls are
painted plain white.
(*Eggshell*, if you
ask my mom.)

There are no
throw pillows,
framed photos, or
cool pieces of art.

All I have is a
twin-size bed,
a dresser, and a
bookcase full of
paperbacks.

My room isn't
anything special.
But it's the one place
I can breathe.

DREAMS

On my corkboard,
there's a calendar
I printed from online

and a photo of
upstate New York,
where I'll live next year.

I'm counting down
the days until
graduation.

Until I can exist
outside the borders
of my bedroom.

NORMAL

Downstairs, I can hear Dad
turn up the volume on the TV.
I remember when he met Dr. Lewis
at our first (and only) family therapy session.
That was years ago. Right after
I got out of the hospital.

The three of us crammed together
on the tiny office couch.
At six foot two,
Dad looked like a giant.
He had just come from
the office and was still
wearing his suit and tie.
(The green-striped tie that
my mom had never liked.)
I could see his five o'clock shadow
and bags under his eyes.

Dr. Lewis stared at Mom.
Mom stared at Dad.
Dad stared at the clock.

When asked how he felt,
Dad looked nervous.
Like a contestant on a game show
scared to give the wrong answer.
*I'm just waiting for things
to be normal again.*

WHEN WERE THINGS NORMAL?

Before I went
to the hospital?

Before I started
high school?

Before I drank
my first beer?

Before I learned
to play clarinet?

Before I could write
my full name?

Before my baby book
was finished?

Before I even
existed?

BEFORE

I know when
things were normal.

Things were normal
before the party.

That party.

THAT PARTY

It was the summer before
I started high school.

I had never gone
to a party that didn't
involve cake and balloons.

If I hadn't been so nervous,
maybe I would have felt
the magic of a summer night.

No school, no parents—
just the moon and music.

HIM

You look lost, he said.

I had left to get a drink
and couldn't find my friends.

He was cute, with curly hair
and sharp green eyes.
The kind you can't forget.

He told me he just graduated
Greenville High. He was going
to college in the fall.

He asked if I wanted to go upstairs.
Away from the music. Just us.

WHAT HAPPENED

He kissed me and
I kissed him back.

Things were fine,
until he pulled me down

and I realized

that this wasn't my bed,
and this wasn't my house,

and I didn't know his name,
but now I was too
embarrassed to ask.

I told him I had to leave.

I told him my friends
were looking for me.

I told him I wasn't ready.

AFTER

I didn't realize I had
been crying until after.
When I saw my red eyes
in the bathroom mirror.

Now I live
every day
in the After.

ELLIE

Ellie texts me:

*You OK? Didn't see
you after lunch.*

Ellie: my best friend
and the only person
(outside of therapy)
who I told about the party.

When I tried to say *rape*,
the word caught in my throat
like a piece of tough meat.

It wasn't a word I could
chew and fully digest.

But she understood anyway,
or at least held my hand.

FRIENDS

In middle school,
we had a friend group:

Ellie, Amber,
Steph, and I.

Ellie was the tough one.
Not afraid to ask a guy out
or sneak a beer for
the first time.

Amber was glamorous.
Always watching makeup
tutorials and using us
as her test subjects.

Steph wore band shirts
and acted like she
didn't care about looks
(even though she did).

I guess I was
the creative one.
The artist. The writer.

BREAKING

Ellie was my only friend
who didn't fade away
after my episode.
My *psychotic break.*

> That's what they called it—
> *a psychotic break.*
> Back in the hospital.
> Back in ninth grade.

The doctors said I had
delusions and was
seeing things.

> And that's why I
> was scared of
> everything.

MESS

I was so confused.
How could I trust
what the doctors said to be true?

I tried to argue.

> *You don't understand.*
> *You don't understand.*

But my words came out
a jumbled mess.
They just sighed and said,

> *You're not making sense.*
> *You're not making sense.*

BENDING

Psychotic break sounds as if
I woke up one day with
shards of white and gray matter
where there used to be a brain.

But to me, it was more like
my mind had been bending.
Things changed before I could
realize what was happening.

PARANOIA

It began with my bedroom windows.

I put newspaper over the glass
a couple weeks after the party.

I just didn't want anyone looking
into my room, seeing my private space.

Over time, I started to actually believe
that people were always watching me,

waiting for a moment of weakness.

DREAD

Every day
in the morning

I woke up convinced
that someone was
out to get me.

That someone
might come by
and take me away.

I started picturing
figures in dark cloaks.

Sometimes I swore
I could see them
lurking in the corners.

Shadows where there
shouldn't be shadows.

HIDE AWAY

When my fear grew
larger, my world
became smaller.

I didn't want to
talk to anyone.
I didn't want to
see my friends or
even go to school.

All I wanted to do
was hide in my room.

KEEP/DITCH

The things I kept:

curtains closed,
door locked,
computer turned off.

The things I got rid of:

movie nights,
texting friends,
family dinners.

SCHOOL

Instead of going to class,
I hid in the bathroom.

I thought the food in
the cafeteria was poisoned.

I didn't tell my teachers
how people were watching
me from my computer.
How I saw lurking shadows
in the corners of their classrooms.

I didn't tell my parents why
I didn't want to go to school.
Or why I was so scared to
even leave my room.

No one seemed safe
enough to talk to.

CONFUSION

My thoughts were like
a long sentence
with no punctuation
or a story with no
beginning or end.

Just

confusion confusion
confusion confusion
confusion confusion
confusion confusion
confusion confusion

FEAR

I couldn't think
straight, so I always
felt scared.

Every day the fear
brewed and bubbled.
Like a cooking pot full
of steaming hot water.

Until eventually,
one day,
it boiled over.

TARGET

When I saw security guards
near my locker,
I knew it was over for me.

I thought they were trying
to take me away to jail,
or maybe some laboratory.

I didn't know the principal
asked them to do locker checks
on all the students.

All I could imagine
was me as their target.

CRISIS

I must have been yelling
and kicking and crying

loud enough for the students
on the second floor to hear me,

because all of a sudden
I was surrounded by faces

with me in the center.

THE DRIVE

Mom's hands shook as she
drove me to the ER.

Dad rested his head on
the passenger-side window.

I was in the back seat, crying.
That's all I remember.

FEAR CONFIRMED

Hospitals are supposed to
make you feel better, right?

But when I was dragged
by my elbows through the
sterile hallways,

all I felt was my fear
of being taken away
finally confirmed.

AFTER THE HOSPITAL

When I got out,
I felt defeated. Tired

from trying to explain myself
to doctors who refused to listen—

who wanted me to shut up
and not ask questions.

Mom tried to find me
a therapist in town.

But they wouldn't take me
once they heard my diagnosis.

I was considered *too much to handle*
by everyone except Dr. Lewis.

He was the first person
to actually listen.

DR. LEWIS

For four sessions,
I couldn't sit down.

I paced his office,
checking for
hidden cameras.

I made sure
no one was
behind the door,

listening in on
our conversation.

But Dr. Lewis
waited for me
to feel comfortable.

And eventually,
I did.

PSYCHOSIS 101, LESSON TWO

There are many
different ways
to experience
psychosis.

And there are
many different
treatment
options.

What works
for one person
won't work
for everyone.

You have to do
what's right
for you.

MEDICATION

I took the pills prescribed.
But I still felt a bit paranoid.
I saw shadows sometimes.

Dr. Lewis said that meds
are never the entire answer,
just a piece of the puzzle.

When I told him I wished
there was a simple solution,
he shook his head and said,

Why view it as a problem?
Recovery is always a process.

GOSSIP

Back at school, students
would stare, but would never
say anything to my face.

I used to feel paranoid
that people were
talking about me.

But now they actually *were* whispering
about me in the hallways.

How was it possible to feel
like the center of attention
when no one would even
look in my direction?

BITE

After my *break,*

parents, teachers, doctors

would handle me
like I was a snake:

gently,

because

I might

just

bite.

ACTUALLY...

Most animals
only bite
humans when
they're scared.

(But people
tend to
forget that.)

GUILTY

I tried to talk to Mom
about the party,
about after.

But when I tried
to talk about
the past,

I always felt
guilty.

Like I was
forcing her
to relive *her*
bad memories

of seeing her
own daughter
go crazy.

HAUNTED

It felt like I was
a haunted object.

Like Annabelle
or a Chucky Doll.

Carrying a curse
my house could never
be rid of.

EASIER

It was easier
to pretend things
were normal.

It was easier
to stay alone in
my room

than to be
anywhere near
my parents.

It was easier
to watch my
friends leave

than try to
explain
what happened.

It was easier
to keep things
to myself.

It was easier
to just stay
silent.

TODAY

Mom keeps a photo
of me from eighth grade
taped to the fridge.

In her perfect world,
I'm still that little girl
in the picture.

We stay up late
watching Netflix in
the living room.

I ask her for advice
about boys and friends
as she strokes my hair.

There are no
awful pauses,
no silence too strong
for us to overcome.

We just talk.

SKIP

I can't wait for school
to finally be over.

I hate spending
eight hours every weekday
stuck in Greenville High.

Sometimes I skip
when Ellie is out sick.

She has stomach issues,
stiff joints, sore muscles...

> (*Etc., etc.* she says when
> people ask her about it.)

But today, I know
she'll be in class.

And that makes
boarding the morning bus
a little bit easier.

ENGLISH, FIRST PERIOD

Ms. Gomez asks the class
if anyone knows what the
answer to number 13 is.

*You're all supposed to graduate
this year and no one will
even guess the answer?!*

The answer is *hyperbole,*
but I keep quiet and
stare down at my desk.

My rule for school is simple:
blend in until the bell rings.

THE WRITER

If I had to pick
a favorite class,
it would be English.

I like to read and
I've been writing my
own stories since
middle school.

I even won a
short story contest
with a $500 cash prize
back in eighth grade.

I used to love to
show my stories to
Mom or send them
to my friends.

But I don't share
my writing with
anyone anymore.

I hide my stories
like a secret.

LUNCH

This time, I get to
the table without
spilling my tray.

But when I sit down,
I can't see Ellie
in the crowd
of T-shirts, sneakers,
and baseball caps.

I pull up my hoodie and
push my hair forward.
My brown waves
frame my face like a
window curtain.

I just want to hide
in plain sight.

NOT FUNNY

On the other side
of the cafeteria table,

two boys from the
lacrosse team
joke around with
their friend. It's Brian,
from my math class.

Brian laughs as they
wrap his sleeves
around his torso,
like a straitjacket.

For a brief second,
he catches my eye.

Which only makes him
laugh harder.

PEP TALK

I finally see Ellie
walking toward me
with her tray in hand.
Her hair sits atop her head,
pulled into a messy bun.
Even though it's almost summer, she's
wearing her favorite
tall black boots.
She rolls her eyes
when she sees the guys.
Gross.

> I wish I could
> blend my colors
> to my surroundings
> like a chameleon.
> I could fade
> right into this table.

Ellie pokes her food
with a plastic fork,
then abandons her plate
for a bag of hot chips.

Ignore them, she says.
They're immature.
We won't remember them
once high school is over.

COLLEGE

Ellie got into
Ithaca College.

Right after her
acceptance letter
came in the mail,
she asked if I would
move with her.

*Upstate New York is
beautiful,* she said.
*And so many writers
live there!*

I couldn't have said
yes any quicker.

I don't plan
to stay stuck
in this town,

especially if Ellie
isn't even around.

PUBLIC SPEAKING, SEVENTH PERIOD

Public speaking:
the worst class
I've ever been
forced to take.

I usually skip and wait outside until the
buses start to pull in.

But this time my teacher
spots me before I can
dip down the hallway.

See me after class,
Ms. Sanders says as
I walk toward my desk
in the back of the room.

PROJECT

Kendall Wilson
sits in the front row
wearing her pink jacket,
no ketchup stain in sight.

I (kind of) listen
to Ms. Sanders talk about
our final project.

We have to split into pairs
and interview each other
in front of the class.

She'll be grading us on
our presentation skills
and *how we engage with
the audience.*

The interview topic:
*What are you
passionate about?*

...

And guess who I'm
paired up with.

KENDALL WILSON

By another name: perfect.

Her nails are
painted peach pink,
without any chips.

She turns in
her homework early
and always
raises her hand.

When Ms. Sanders
pairs us together,
the corners of
Kendall's lips
curve down.

But only for
a moment.

SHRINK

When the bell rings,
Ms. Sanders stops me
before I can escape.

Under her long blonde bangs,
I see her eyes narrow.
I can't tell if she's mad or concerned.

Her heels click as she
walks toward her desk.

I pull up a chair
and sit with my arms and legs crossed.

Trying to make myself
as small as possible.

MOUTH CLOSED, HEAD DOWN

*Do you know that
you're failing my class?*

I don't say a word.
I keep my mouth
closed and
my head down.

*You always skip class.
And when you're here,
you never raise your hand...*

Mouth closed,
head down.

*...and you never take part
in any activities...*

Mouth closed,
head down.

She sighs, and
I know I've heard
that sigh before.

It means I'm being
too difficult.

NEXT

I wait for the
next criticism,
but instead, her
voice softens.

*Are you doing
alright, Mara?*

I'm never
exactly sure
how to answer
this question.

So I don't.

WORST WORDS

Then she says
the worst words that
can come from
a teacher.

Mara, if you don't pass
this class, you can't graduate.
Do you understand?

Immediately the fear
spikes again—

>   but I think this time,
>   anyone would be scared.

STUCK

Graduation
is all I've been
thinking about
since ninth grade.

That cap and gown
is my escape
from the past.

How can I
move forward now?

HOPELESS

Ms. Sanders says
I need to try to ace
my final project.

I paired you with my
star student, Kendall.
Hopefully she can
help you.

She says there's still
a chance I can pass
with a 60 percent.

But I feel 100 percent
hopeless.

MEMORIAL

I stand in my driveway
for over an hour.

This is my house.
This is where I live.

Then why does it feel fake,
like a model home?

Why does walking in
feel like an intrusion?

How can you live in a
house that's more
like a museum—

a memorial to what
a home could have been?

DISAPPOINTMENT

Mom sits at the table,
coffee cup in hand.

Are you hungry?
I made veggie dip.

Today of all days,
she has to be nice?

Her smile
makes me want
to fall to my knees
and apologize.

To say *I'm sorry,*
again and again,

for being such a
disappointment.

INSTEAD

I tell her I ate a big lunch
and disappear upstairs.

ALONE

I lock my
bedroom door
behind me.

I want to be
alone.

I don't want to
put on a show

of

everything's fine,
everything's normal.

FOR NOW

For the first time
in a while, I can't
stop thinking about
my windows.

The curtains are
always closed.
But still...

Wouldn't it be safer
if I covered them
in newspaper—
just in case
someone is
watching?

There's a bin
downstairs with
newspapers and
old magazines that
I could grab.
But instead, I
squeeze my palms
together, like
I'm holding my
own hand.

Eventually,
the urge passes.

PSYCHOSIS 101, LESSON THREE

Dr. Lewis said
that stress can trigger
symptoms.

*Try not to get
overwhelmed.*

     That's easier said
     than done.

     But sometimes
     it still helps
     just to breathe

     in and out,
     in and out.

PLAN

Dr. Lewis doesn't give me
a hard time
when I tell him about
failing public speaking.

He doesn't sigh
or shake his head.

He doesn't even
press his lips together,

the way my mom does
when she hears bad news
or drinks something sour.

He only asks,
*Well, what do you
want to do about that?*

MEETING

After school the next day,
I meet up with Kendall
in the school courtyard.

When I arrive,
she's already
sitting at the picnic table.

She sticks out her hand.
Hi, I'm Kendall Wilson.

Oh, I know.
Between the morning
announcements and
her run for student council,
it's hard not to have
heard her name.

(I wonder if
she even remembers
the ketchup incident.)

Her smile looks painful,
like she's holding it too tight.

It's Mara, right?

IDEAS

I remember what
she said at lunch
the other day.

My stomach knots,
but I smile and nod.

Before I can think further,
she pulls out a laptop,
two notebooks, and
a three-ring binder.

Ready to get to work.

TALK/LISTEN

Kendall is the type
who can talk for days.

I have lots of ideas!
I want to be a journalist,
so I know all about
how interviews go.

We have to keep it
interesting, but classy.
And oh—what were
you going to wear?

It has to be professional.
I'll send you my
Girl Boss Instagram
for inspiration.

If Kendall is the type
who talks and talks,
I guess I'm the type
who sits and listens.

GONE

Kendall wants a big show,

but I don't want to talk.

I don't want to be seen.

If I could take my picture
out of the yearbook,
I would—

Erase myself from
Greenville High's memory.

And erase Greenville High
from mine.

UPDATE

Ellie laughs when
I tell her about
Kendall's ideas.

If you're not careful,
she'll dress you up
like a doll in one of
her preppy jackets.

I don't want
to be Kendall's
puppet.

But maybe I could
update my closet,
just a little bit.

SHOPPING TRIP

Ellie is surprised
that I want to
go shopping.

(To be fair,
I'm usually not
the one who
wants to go
places.)

Remember how
we used to always
go thrifting back
in eighth grade?

Right.
That's me.

The girl who
used to do things.

THRIFTING

We head downtown
to a thrift store

with rows of jeans and jackets,
handbags and boots.

I laugh as Ellie
runs down the aisles

and tries to fit kid's shoes
over her size-nine feet.

I remember why
I used to like shopping.

PROM DRESS

Ellie finds
ballroom dresses
in the back.

She laughs.
Oh my gosh,
check out these
shoulder pads.

I pull a blue dress
from the rack
with tulle that
trails to the floor.

But instead
of giggling,
Ellie's eyes
widen.

That would look
so good with
your dark hair.
It's a perfect
prom dress.

Prom? Please.
She knows
I don't go
to parties.

NEW-ISH

I leave the prom dress,
but I buy a new blazer
and pair of sandals.

> Well, they aren't
> actually new.
> *Pre-loved,* as the
> store sign says.

But they're new to me.
That's what matters.

SLEEPOVER

Ellie's been asking
me to sleep over
ever since
she got her own room
once her sister moved.

This time,
I accept the invite.

    These are the moments
    Dr. Lewis tells me
    to appreciate.

I can imagine him saying,

    Three years ago,
    you wouldn't feel safe
    sleeping anywhere
    without the doors
    double locked.

    See how far
    you've come?

But I still look
over my shoulder
when we walk back
to the car.

SMOKE

We smoke weed
in the park behind
Ellie's house.

Well, Ellie smokes
while I pull wildflowers
from the ground.

She hands over
the joint to be polite,
but she knows
I'll decline.

I don't want to
get paranoid.

DANDELION

Make a wish.

I hold a
dandelion
between my
fingers.

Ellie giggles
softly, like a
secret.

As the sun
starts to set
around us,

this tiny
moment
feels like
magic.

BUT...

The fear
still lingers
in the back
of my mind.

Like smoke
left after
Ellie's joint
burns out.

It doesn't
bother me
like it
used to.

But I know
it's still there,
in the air.

PARENTS

At Ellie's house,
her mom brings us
a bowl of popcorn
while we stream
a new horror movie.

I want to ask
if her mom ever lies
to her coworkers
about how often Ellie
goes to the doctor.

Or does her dad ever
tell his friends
that she's *doing great*,
when really she's
in bed, in pain?

Do they ever treat her
like she might break?

Or do they ever
not know
what to say?

HORROR MOVIE

Ellie watches
without flinching.

Blood, guts, guns—
nothing bothers her.

Unlike me—
I cover my eyes

and watch from
between my fingers.

NOT LIKE THE MOVIES

In Hollywood,
people with psychosis
go on murder sprees.

Men who hallucinate
shoot up buildings.
Women with delusions
torture their lovers.

But I never wanted
to even squash a spider.

PSYCHOSIS 101, LESSON FOUR

Dr. Lewis
once said,

*Psychosis does not
make someone
more likely
to be violent.*

*Actually, they are
more likely to be
the victim
of violence.*

Is it too much
to ask
to be neither?

Dr. Lewis asks
what I'm going to
talk about
during the interview.

If there's one thing
Kendall is
passionate about,
it's drama.

She can't stop
talking about:
Her big plans
for the future.
Her hot boyfriend.
How to go
viral on the
internet.

Me? I don't have
anything
to share.

NOTHING LEFT

What can I say
about myself
that hasn't already
been said
in ninth grade,

whispered
between students
in the hallway?

> *(She's psychotic—*
> *actually psychotic!)*

My story has already
been shared,

and now there's
nothing left.

DR. LEWIS'S ADVICE

*People might know
about you, but they
don't really know
who you are.*

*They might have
witnessed a dark moment
from a distance.*

*But they have never
seen what makes you
happy, what you're
passionate about.*

MEMORY BOXES

Mom raises
her eyebrows
when I ask if she
still has my award
from seventh grade.

She doesn't ask
what for. Instead,
she helps me shuffle
through boxes of
things she stored away
in our basement.

My drawings from
first grade.
Old school photos.
A+ projects
with gold stars.

I never realized
how many things
she saved.

OUR DAY TOGETHER

Finally, we find
my award certificate
pressed in a
purple envelope,
along with my
original story.

This is the most time
Mom and I
have spent together
in three years—

on our hands and knees,
rooting through papers.

I'm sure she has
better things to do
on a sunny Saturday
afternoon.

But she doesn't seem
to mind.

And surprisingly,
neither do I.

TURTLE

I'm surprised
when Mom says,

*You wanted to spend
that prize money
on a turtle,
remember?*

I laugh.
Oh yeah.

I went through a reptile phase
when I was 13.

I wanted a turtle.
Mom wouldn't
buy me one.

We start putting
the boxes back
up on the shelf.

A lot has changed,
she says.

Yeah, it has.

POTENTIAL

My award-winning story
isn't all that amazing.

It has silly characters
and odd plot holes.

But I guess the judges
saw potential.

WRITER'S BLOCK

I haven't written much
in the past few months.

But seeing that award
gets me to open my notebook.

I lie on my stomach
with a pen in hand.

I try to brainstorm
new story ideas,

but all I can do is
drag the pen across the paper,

doodling circles
and spirals, squares
and coils.

INSPIRATION

I pin the award on the
corkboard, next to
my calendar and
photo of New York.

I know it looks silly,
but it might spark
some inspiration.

SECOND MEETING

Kendall and I meet again
to go over the details
of our final project.

If I've struggled to find
things to say, then
Kendall has been having
the opposite problem.

She doesn't seem to
mind sharing

(or bragging).

NOT-SO-HUMBLE BRAGS

*You should ask me
questions about college.
I'm really passionate
about education.*

*You know, I've been
accepted to Stanford,
but I'm holding out for
Harvard or Yale.*

*In five years,
I'll be an intern
at Fox News,
or maybe CNN—*

*Oh, and married to
my boyfriend.
We're practically
engaged already.*

*Are you writing this
down?*

JUST WRITE

Eventually, Kendall asks
what I want to talk about
in my interview.

*Let's get into all the
juicy details*, she says.

When I tell her
I want to talk about
writing, she doesn't
seem impressed.

*You like writing?
That's it?
What's your
five-year plan?
Who have you
published with?*

I pick at my nails
under the table.
(Mom used
to hate when I
did that.)

*Nothing. No one.
I don't have a
five-year plan.
Writing just makes
me happy.*

She doesn't seem
to understand.

QUESTIONS

Kendall talks so fast,
I can hardly
make out her
questions.

> *Can't you find
> another thing
> to talk about—*
>
> *something actually
> interesting?*
>
> *What college
> are you going to,
> Ivy or public?*
>
> *Do you have
> a boyfriend?*
>
> *Are you part
> of any clubs?*
>
> *Do you know
> anyone famous?*

NOISE

I try to answer her,
but she doesn't seem
to care about my
responses at all.

(I heard Mom say once
that some people just like
to hear themselves talk.)

If we ever want to
finish this project,
I'm going to have to
speak louder
to be heard over all
the noise.

AGREEMENT

Kendall, slow down!

My voice projects
louder than it has
in a while.

It sounds scratchy,
like a machine that
needs to be oiled.

I get Kendall to stop
talking long enough
for us to agree on a set
of questions.

But she still doesn't
seem impressed.

*I just hope these questions
aren't too bland,* she says.
*We're being graded on
engaging the audience—
not putting them to sleep.*

THIS WEEK

I go to every
single class.

(I even raise
my hand in English.)

In public speaking,
Ms. Sanders
is glad that I'm
attending.

*Looking forward
to seeing your
interview, Mara.*

*I'm glad you're
turning things
around.*

> *Me too,*
> I think, but I
> don't say it
> out loud.

PRACTICE

I practice my interview
with Ellie after school.

She pretends
to be Kendall while
asking me questions.

She even puts on
a big, bright grin.

Afterward, she jokes
that holding that smile
made her jaw hurt.

*It must take practice
to be that fake.*

> I shove her lightly
> on the shoulder.

> *Don't be mean.*

> (But I can't help
> laughing.)

NEW YORK

We take a break
to sip lemonade
and watch our
favorite sitcom.

One character
is about to go
to art school
in New York.

Every time Ellie
hears *New York*
mentioned,
she squeals.

*I can't wait to
move to Ithaca!
Aren't you
excited?*

I'm excited,
but scared.

I hope I can get
that diploma
in my hand.

SUPPORT

Ellie doesn't have to ask
If I'm worried about
the interview.

She can already tell
by the way I'm
picking at my nails.

Don't worry, she says.
*I'll sneak out of math
so I can cheer you on
from the doorway.*

That's why she's
my best friend.
She knows exactly
what I need.

NERVOUS

In seventh period,
students start
to present their
final projects.

Ms. Sanders sits
at her desk, watching
with her notes in hand.

The first student will
interview their partner
for five minutes.
Then they'll switch.

The first person
mumbles when they
ask their questions
and keeps looking
around, distracted.

I guess everyone is
a little nervous.

TOGETHER

When I come home,
Mom is watching a
sea life documentary
while folding Dad's clothes.

(I'll never understand
why he can't fold
his own laundry or
do his own dishes.)

I take a seat on the
other end of the couch
and watch for a while.

There's a gap of
space between us,
but we're still
sitting together.

TALK

Mom tests the waters
and asks how
school is.

I watch the
dolphins squeak
on screen,

communicating
with no effort
at all.

Meanwhile,
I can't think of
one thing to say.

FINE

School's fine,
is all I can
come up with.

I don't tell her
I'm presenting my
final project
tomorrow.

I don't tell her
that I might not
graduate if I
fail this.

Right now,
things are calm
between us.

Why add
any waves?

ALERT

Before I go to bed,
I get a text from Ellie.

> *Hey! I'm so sorry
> but I feel really sick
> & don't think I'll
> make it to school
> tomorrow.*
>
> *Don't worry—
> you'll kill it!*

Now I'm not feeling
so confident.

PANIC

Try not to panic.

That's what
Dr. Lewis
would say.

But my heart
is already
pounding.

It feels like
ice is trailing
down my spine.

I close my eyes.

Count to three.
Breathe in.

Count to three.
Breathe out.

GOOGLE SEARCH HISTORY

Good interview examples

> Best public speaking tips

Best tea to relax nerves

> Calming music playlist

How to nail a final project

> How to stop overthinking

What to do if you can't fall asleep

> Does counting sheep work?

How to sleep while anxious

> How to feel confident

DRESSED UP

You look nice,
Mom says the
next morning.

For the first time
in a while, my hair
is out of my face
and pulled back
in a ponytail.

I even used some
of the makeup
my grandma
bought for my
birthday last year.

I like your blazer,
she says, and
I smile.

OUTFITS

Kendall comes to class
in a full pantsuit,
with her hair in a bun.

As if she is
a news reporter
in a beauty pageant.

I look down at my shoes,
which now seem
a little dirty—

and why does my blazer
keep sliding off my
shoulders?

IT'S TIME

Ms. Sanders
calls our names.

Kendall jumps
out of her seat.

She walks swiftly to
the front of the room.

My legs wobble
as I walk forward.

I feel faint, as if I
haven't eaten in a while.

Ellie would tell me
to stay strong.

But I feel only as strong
as a feather.

EYES ON ME

Kendall sits
perfectly,
ready to perform.

But even her
huge smile and
perfect teeth

can't distract me
from all of the eyes
staring at me.

I feel like a
mannequin on display
for the whole
class to stare at.

It takes all my energy
to make my legs
walk to the front
of the room.

BREATHE

The good thing about
breathing exercises
is that you can

count and breathe,
        count and breathe,
count and breathe,
        count and breathe.

Without anyone knowing
what you're doing.

Breathe in.

Hold your breath
for four counts,

1
        2
                3
                        4

                        and
                        breathe out.

10/10

I keep telling myself,
I can do this.
I can do this.

I ask Kendall all of
her preapproved
questions

about debate team
and drama class
and her run for
student body
president.

She answers
without a moment
of hesitation
and beams
across the room
like an actress.

10/10
performance.

AFTERWARD

She's still grinning
toward the audience
when I hear her growl
under her breath,

Speak louder.
Don't mess this
up, got it?

When she turns in
my direction,
her glare lets me
know she's serious.

MY TURN

Count my breath,
try not to panic.

In a few minutes,
it will all be over.

In a few minutes,
my breathing will be
back to normal again.

In a few minutes,
I'll be one step
closer to graduation.

I can do this.

I can do this.

I can do this.

THE BEGINNING

It starts off well.

Kendall introduces me
as an aspiring author

and asks me
the first question
we came up with:

*What do you like most
about writing?*

My voice starts off soft,
but I clear my throat
and continue.

*You don't have to be
perfect to be a writer.
It's okay to mess up
and rewrite some parts.*

*It's okay to start
writing a story, even
if you don't know
the ending yet.*

FOCUS

Even though we
switched roles,
it's clear that Kendall
still wants to
be the focus.

After my first answer,
she cuts me off
and dives into
her next question.

Are you concerned
that you might never
be successful?

WOUNDED

We never agreed
on that question,
I'm sure of it.

I try to respond,
but before I can
finish another
sentence, she's
already bored
with my answer.

She fires another
question.

This time,
it hits like a bullet.

*What's it like
to be psychotic?*

SHOCK

I should say
something,
anything.

But my lips feel
cemented shut.

My whole body
tenses up.

And even
though my feet
are on the
ground,

I feel
completely
detached.

AUDIENCE

Now everyone
looks super focused.

Finally, Kendall
has captured her
audience.

PANDORA'S BOX

Kendall glares,
fully expecting
an answer.

Finally,
I start to speak.

*I don't, um...
can we move on?*

I want to talk about
how I started writing.

Or what inspires me
when I'm stuck
with writer's block.

But now that she
has mentioned
psychosis,

the unwritten rule
of polite silence
has been broken.

And everyone's
curiosities
come out.

COMMENTS

A girl in the back
raises her hand.

*Does psychosis
make you creative,
like van Gogh?*

      A guy in a baseball cap
      chimes in:

      *No, it makes you
      want to kill people,
      like the Joker.*

A girl who I used to do
Girl Scouts with says,

*I heard that once
you snap, you're
never the same.*

      A guy I've known since
      second grade mentions,

      *I had an uncle
      who was schizophrenic
      and super weird.*

OUT LOUD

I know this is
what people
think and say,

but usually,
it's done
in murmurs.

Tiny whispers
here and there.

Settle down!
Ms. Sanders
says.

But the
presentation
is already
wrecked.

And no amount
of breathing
in and out
can fix this.

RUN

I don't think.
I just run.

Out of the
classroom,

out of the
hallway,

out of the
school.

        If I could,
        I would run

        out of this
        town,

        out of this
        country,

        out of
        this world.

REFLECTION

I run home and
go straight up
to my room.

I look in the mirror
above my dresser.

There are smudges
all around my eyes
from my mascara.

My first thought is that
I look insane.

Well, ha-ha.
I guess I am.

SICK DAYS

I don't go to school
the next day,

or the day after,

or the day after.

I tell my parents
I have the flu.

My dad just
shakes his head.

I don't think
they buy it—

but what does
it matter?

IGNORE

Mom knocks,
but I don't answer.

Ellie texts,
but I don't respond.

Dr. Lewis calls,
but I delete his
voicemail.

I just want
to hit ignore
again and again.

I just want to
put the world
on pause
for a moment.

FAMILY DINNER

Mom forces me
to come downstairs
so we can all pick at
our baked chicken
together.

Dad checks his phone
under the table.
Mom rests her chin
on her hand.
I stir my mashed potatoes
with my spoon.

Families shouldn't
eat dinner together
when the only sound
is silverware
scraping on the plate.

EXPLODE

Mom breaks the silence,
like glass shattering
on the kitchen floor.

Both Dad and I sit up,
startled.

*I just got a call from the
school guidance counselor...*

Dad taps his fingers
on the table. I wait.

*She's concerned that
Mara's been skipping class...*

She doesn't look at me.
She just stares at her plate.

*She said, with her grades,
she might not graduate.*

DAD SPEAKS

My dad,
who has made a
hobby out of
staying silent,
now has a million
things to say.

*What? How could
this happen? We
raised you to take
responsibility.
We raised you to
work hard, not skip
class and slack off.*

*What were you
thinking?*

*I'm so
disappointed.*

RELEASE

Just like Kendall,
he never pauses
to let me respond.

He wants me to
sit and listen.

To witness his
pent-up anger
finally release.

When he yells
about my grades,
I know what
he really wants
to say:

*Why did you
have to go ruin
everything?*

MOM RESPONDS

Scott, calm down.
I'm sure she already feels bad.
We can figure this out.

We can look into summer school.
Or maybe talk to her teachers.
It sounds like it's only
one class she's failing.

I've been worried about
how silent she's been.
Perhaps we should ask
the therapist...

INVISIBLE

They talk like they've
forgotten I'm sitting here.

Once again, I'm the
center of attention

that no one can even
bear to look at.

But I'm here. I exist.

And I'm tired,
so tired, of people

speaking about me,
speaking over me.

Speaking as if
I don't have
a voice of my own.

Maybe I don't
want to always
be invisible.

Maybe I don't
want to always be
the quiet listener.

SCREAM

For the first time
in three years,
I scream.

And scream

And scream.

And scream.

And

the

whole

room

freezes.

JUST A PERSON

Tonight, no one dares
disturb the crazy lady
locked in her
bedroom.

I don't want
to always be silent,
to blend in with
the rug and curtains.

But I don't want to
have to scream either.

I just want them
to listen for once.

Why can't they see me
as not invisible,
not crazy,

just a person?

MOURNING

The next morning,
I find myself staring
at my reflection again.

How do I stop
mourning the person
I was supposed to be?

How do I stop missing
the girl who is now only
a picture on the
refrigerator?

PSYCHOSIS 101, LESSON FIVE

Reach out for support
before things get bad.

That's what everyone
always says.

The doctors at the hospital.
School counselors.
Teachers. Dr. Lewis.

Always ask for help
when you're struggling.

> (But what if you're
> scared they'll turn
> you away?)

TEXTS

My phone
vibrates.
Another text
from Ellie.

> *How did it go!!??*
>
> *You there?*
>
> *Hey, I heard
> what happened.
> Call me.*
>
> *Are you okay?*
>
> *Can you please
> text me back.*
>
> *MARA?
> Come on.*

I should call.
I know I'm being
a bad friend.

But I just
feel
exhausted.

VISITOR

Mom knocks on my door.
Please, can I come in?

*Ellie called. She's worried.
And I know you missed your
last therapy appointment.*

So what, now she wants
to talk? To say something
beyond *How was your day* or
Have you eaten dinner?

I don't answer,
but she doesn't give up.

*Please, Mara.
Give me a chance
to prove to you
that I care.*

*I don't want us to make
the same mistakes again.*

I'm not sure
what I'm opening
myself up to.

But I take the risk
and let her in.

MOM SAYS...

*I'm sorry for
what happened
at dinner.*

*I don't
always know
what to say.*

I open my mouth,
but no words
come out.

I guess I don't
always know
what to say
either.

FINALLY

Before I lose my nerve
and stop myself
from speaking the truth,
I finally ask her why.

Why did they
take me to the hospital
before even asking me
what was wrong?

Why did they act weird
when I tried to talk
about it afterward?

Why did they treat me
like a family secret?

Why were they always
so quiet?

HER SIDE

When the school
called about
my breakdown
back in ninth grade,
she panicked.

She didn't want
to talk it through.

She wanted
a quick fix
so we could all
be happy again.

She wanted her
daughter back,

       but I had always
       been there.

       *I'm sorry it took me
       so long to see that.*

HUG

For the
first time
in forever,

we give
each other
a real hug.

(Not a half-hug
or some kind
of awkward
embrace.)

I almost cry
from how
nice it feels

to be supported
by another
person.

To lean on her
shoulder,

if only
for a moment.

BACK IN THERAPY

I have so much
that I want to say,
but no energy to say it.

I let Dr. Lewis speak first.

I missed you last week.
I'm glad to see you back.

I know I don't
have to talk about
what happened.

But maybe I'll feel better
once I get it out
of my system.

JUDGED

When I tell Dr. Lewis
what happened in
seventh period,
he says he's proud.

Proud?
I can't imagine why.

I feel like I
humiliated myself.

And worst of all?
Everyone in class
will graduate,
and I'll be stuck here.

Nothing was your fault,
he says.

Kendall used you.
Your classmates
were very rude.

I shrug.

> *I guess. But at*
> *the end of the day,*
> *I'm still the one*
> *everybody judges.*

SPEECHLESS

Dr. Lewis
crosses his arms
and leans back
in his chair.

*Does everybody
judge you, or do you
judge yourself?*

> I don't know
> what to say
> to that.

MY QUESTION

I answer with
another question.

A question that
I never wanted
to ask out loud.

It's something
I've been wondering
for a while.

When I open my
mouth, the words fall
out like marbles,

spilling out without
any control.

> *Do you think I'm weak*
> *because I lost my mind*
> *after some silly party?*

HIS ANSWER

*No. You're not weak.
Your brain was trying
to deal with distress.*

*It wasn't just some
silly party. You
were assaulted.*

*Lots of people
experience psychosis
after something
like that happens.*

*That has nothing
to do with weakness.*

*It takes strength
to deal with all
you've been through.*

WARMTH

Hearing those words
feels like sipping
tea with honey
when you have
a sore throat.

Sure, tea won't
cure your cold.

But it might just
soothe the burn.

SAME, BUT DIFFERENT

Back home, I stare at
my award certificate.

I feel like a different person
than the girl from back then.

But I am the same person.

I have the same hands
and the same feet.

I have the same smile
and the same dimples.

I have the same brain
and the same heart.

I just changed.
Everybody does.

But I'll always be me.

WHEN WERE THINGS NORMAL?

Maybe normal
never existed.

Maybe back then
was just different.

Maybe it's okay
that things changed.

Maybe it's okay
that I've changed.

THANK YOU

Finally, I call Ellie.

She's mad that
I didn't text her back.

I know she was worried.
I tell her I'm sorry.

I'm so glad that
she's my best friend.

I thank her for not
disappearing like the other
girls in our group.

Are you doing okay?
she asks. *All this
touchy-feely stuff
is freaking me out.*

       Yeah, I am.
       I actually am.

       At least for now.

       That's all
       I can ask for.

APOLOGY

Ellie says she's
feeling better.
She'll be back
in school tomorrow.

She might feel fine,
but I feel awful.
I can't believe I forgot
that she's been home sick.

I slap my hand on my
forehead. *Oh my God.*
I'm so sorry, Ellie.
I should have asked.

But Ellie doesn't
sound mad.

Yeah, you should have.
But it's okay.

Sometimes it's hard
to talk when you're
struggling.

ACCEPTANCE

I ask Ellie why
we stayed
friends, even after
all the others left.

She laughs.
You're cool,
I guess. And I happen to
not be a jerk.

She pauses for a moment,
like she's considering
something.

And I know how
it feels to get sick,

and suddenly
it's like you're not
normal enough
for other people
to accept.

So thanks for
accepting me too,
I guess.

GOING BACK

I don't know what's
waiting for me
back at school.

We only have a
few more weeks this year

of buses and late bells
and getting detention.

If I manage to graduate,
I don't think I'll miss
any of it.

(But stranger things
have happened.)

BETTER

Before I leave for school,
I catch my mom
in the kitchen.

She's making her
morning cup of coffee
before work.

Dad has already left
so it's just the two of us.

I stare down at my sandals.
I'm sorry that I shut you out.

We both ignored each other.
We both were scared.

But things can always
get better again.

WORK

Mom's eyes start to
water. She gives me
a small smile.

She's not sure what
to say. I'm not sure
what to say either.

It's weird.
It's awkward.
But that's okay.

We're going to have to
practice being open
with each other.

And I'm willing to
put in the work.

THOUGHTS

I feel okay
walking into school,

but I still can't help
but dread seventh period.

I can only imagine
the things people
might be saying.

Or maybe no one
is talking about it.

And even if they were,
their opinions
wouldn't make
a difference.

NOT OVER YET

Before I take my seat,
Ms. Sanders calls me
to her desk.

She apologizes
for not stopping
Kendall sooner.

*Outing someone's
personal struggles is not
what this class is about.*

She offers to let me
redo my interview
sometime after class

and says she can just
interview me herself.
The school year isn't over.

There can still be a
cap and gown
in my near future.

ANGER

Kendall sits by herself
in the front of the class.

It's the first time
I've seen her quiet.

It occurs to me
that she might also
feel embarrassed.

After class, she comes
to my desk.

Her eyes are puffy
and her face is red.

She's not smiling like
Miss America.

(She's not smiling
in the slightest.)

BLAME

Thanks for nothing, Mara.

Ms. Sanders said
that my questions were
inappropriate.

Now my straight-A
streak is ruined.

She sounds mad, but
her words are lacking
any confidence.

Between the two of us,
I'm not the one she should
be disappointed with.

And I think we both
know it.

WALK AWAY

This time,
I don't feel the
need to run.

But I do
walk away.

I have more
important
things to do

than listen
to Kendall
talk again.

SUNLIGHT

When I get home,
I find a note on
the counter.

My parents went
hiking to enjoy
the nice weather.

It's almost June,
almost the official
start of summer.

I can see the sunlight
peek through my
bedroom curtains.

For the first time
in a long time,
I let the drapes
hang wide open.

BLOOM

Every time I walk home,
I see my neighborhood.

But from the window,
everything looks different.

I see a row of
brick-red townhouses.

I see porches with
potted plants and
waving flags.

I see the spot by
my neighbor's house
where I fell and
chipped my tooth
in second grade.

I see our own front yard,
with my mom's
little garden.

The flowers she planted
are just starting
to sprout up.

It will be nice to see
them bloom.

THAT'S IT!

I jump up and grab
my notebook.

I flip to a new page
without any doodles.

The story I should write
is so obvious.

How could I not see it?

It's my story.

How I survived
the party.

How I managed
psychosis.

How I'm learning
to heal.

It's my story.

And only I
can tell it right.

NEW AGAIN

I write like I'm running
a marathon.

It's slow at first.
I keep overthinking
every sentence, every word.

Does that sound good?
Does that make sense?

But then words start to flow,
and when I'm finally done,
I feel like I just shed
a layer of skin.

My words feel bare.
New again.

PROM

Ellie goes to prom
with a boy she's been
talking about for weeks.

I'm not going.
It's just not my thing.

But I take
a million pictures of
Ellie with her hair curled
in her electric-blue dress.

She jokes that I'm
being such a mom,

but I know she wants
to save this moment.

REDO

Ms. Sanders and I
stay after class,
ready for my
interview.

I hand her a list
of the questions
Kendall was
supposed to ask.

Are you ready?
she asks.

Yes. Finally.

TAKE TWO

Ms. Sanders asks the
questions one by one
while she jots notes
on her clipboard.

It feels so strange to
speak about myself.

But I know these questions.
I've practiced my posture.
I've memorized my answers.

And I feel safe to
finally speak.

HOW LONG HAVE YOU BEEN WRITING?

I started writing stories
when I was six or seven.
My mom was an interior designer,
and I wanted to be creative like her.

So I started writing stories
on the back of my homework.
I loved building worlds and
creating characters.

Back then, everything I wrote
was written in crayon.
But my work has grown a lot
since then, and so have I.

DO YOU HAVE ANY FUTURE PLANS?

After graduation, I'm moving
to upstate New York
to focus on writing
and support my friend,
who got into her dream college.

To be honest, most of my
future plans are yet to be
determined. I'm not going to
college just yet. I don't have it
all figured out just yet.

But like any good book,
I'm excited to see
where the next chapter leads.

DO YOU HAVE ADVICE FOR OTHER WRITERS?

*Nothing you write will ever
be perfect. But you can
rewrite your draft and make
the changes you want.
Try not to overwhelm yourself.
If you feel your fingers
tighten around your pen,
give yourself a break.*

*Writing can be lonely.
You might spend a lot of time
by yourself, with only
your notebook or laptop
as company.*

*So call a friend. Take a walk.
Go shopping. Watch a movie.
Let yourself breathe.*

SKILLS

I use all the
tips and tricks
I read online.

I sit upright,
feet planted firmly
on the floor.

I make sure not to
shake my foot
or tap my fingers.

I try to pause
at the right time
and not say *um*.

When I forget
what to say, I pause
and read the room.

Once my thoughts
are settled,
I start again.

That's the most
important skill:

knowing when
to stop and reflect.

A+

I cry when Ms. Sanders
hands me her notes,
with a huge *A+*
written in red pen.

I cry before I can
even think to feel embarrassed
for crying about
a silly red letter.

Congratulations,
she says. *That was*
wonderfully done.

You were aware of
your body language
and your delivery
was spot-on.

I cry and I smile
and I laugh.

I didn't think
I could do all those
things at once.

LOOKING UP

I go to all my therapy
appointments.

Mom and I watch
a movie together.

I even talk to Dad
for more than five minutes.

> I don't know what the
> future holds.

> But things in the present
> are looking up.

LAST DAY

On the last day of school,
no one throws their
homework in the air.

No one starts screaming
or blasting music.
No one starts dancing
in the hallways, or
cursing out their teachers.

It's not like the movies
(most things aren't).

But there's still a
fun feeling in the air.

Like something
new and exciting
is about to happen.

MEMORIES

Well.
Today's the day.

Mom cries when she
sees me in my
graduation gown.

Even Dad chokes up
a bit. *I'm proud of
you, Mara.*

I don't even need a
photo. I know I'll
remember this.

GRADUATION

The ceremony drags on
for hours and hours.

Half the class forgets
which way to walk.
Several girls in heels
trip over their gowns.

I smile to myself.
Oh well. That's high school.
Sometimes it's a mess.

At the end of the day,
we made it through.
We graduated.

ONWARD

A sea of black gowns
floods the hallways.

The ceremony is over
and all the grads
are rushing out.

Ready to start their
new lives at a new job
or a new school.

I'm excited for my
future too. Going to
New York with Ellie,

figuring things out
with my best friend
by my side.

But I just might
miss Greenville

(only a little).

TWO GRADUATES

Congrats, graduate!
Ellie screams when
she sees me.

I smile and
push her shoulder.
Congrats yourself!

*Are you excited
to finally get out
of here?* she asks.

I laugh. *Yeah, yeah.
But maybe we can
come back and visit.*

She throws her
hair back. *Fine.
Only if you'll
buy the train tickets.*

MOMENT

Ellie and I sit on her bed.
Both pairs of our fancy heels
have been kicked
to the floor.

We dig into a bag
of chips Ellie snagged
from the kitchen.

For now there's nothing
to worry about,
nothing to fear

(even with the windows
open and the door
unlocked).

This feeling won't
last forever.

But for the moment,
it's mine.

PSYCHOSIS 101, LESSON SIX

Recovery doesn't
have to mean that
everything will always
be okay.

Sometimes recovery
means going at
your own speed.

Sometimes recovery
means finding the
support you need.

Sometimes recovery
means you survive
and keep surviving.

CELEBRATION

Ellie mentions
that there's going to be
an after-party at
someone's house.

The thought of a
high school party
still makes my
stomach twist into
a thousand knots.

I'm not ready for that.

Ellie smiles and
raises her can of Coke.
*Then let's have
our own little
celebration.*

CHEERS

Cheers to
graduation.

Cheers to
friendships.

Cheers to
new beginnings.

Cheers to
surviving.

WANT TO KEEP READING?

If you liked this book, check out another book
from West 44 Books:

SICK GIRL SECRETS
BY ANNA RUSSELL

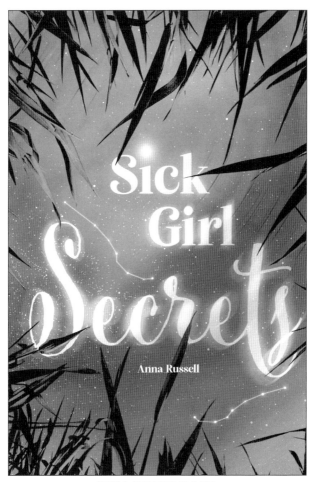

ISBN: 9781978595453

Life Under Glass

If you took a sample
of my life,
put it under glass,
peered at it with a
microscope:

things on the outside
wouldn't seem so different
from yours.

I'm this
        "normal"
girl.

I have a mom.
        A dad.

They're not together anymore,
        but it's not so bad.

Look   a little   closer.

I have a mom
        (who works
        day and night
        to pay for my
        surgeries, medicines,
        appointments,
        ...and more...).

I have a dad
      (who moved to Arizona
      after I got sick and
      I haven't seen him
      in two years).

      Look   a little   closer.

I have a caretaker,
      Mrs. C
      (because I can't take care
      of myself).

      Look closer.

I am this
      "normal"
girl
      (on the outside).

But inside,
      I am broken.

Closer.

Here's the secret of my life:

You have to
splice it open,

        dissect
        the cells.

Microscopic,
     miniscule,
        nanosized.

It's a little different
when you zoom in.

        (I don't want anybody
        to zoom in.)

CHECK OUT MORE BOOKS AT:
www.west44books.com

An imprint of Enslow Publishing

WEST **44** BOOKS™

ABOUT THE AUTHOR

Mel Mallory is a writer and mental health advocate. She has a B.A. in Women and Gender Studies and a minor in English. Her work is influenced by her own experience being disabled and living with psychosis. She currently lives in Maryland with her two guinea pigs. You can find her at www.melmallory.com.